In Distress

Mimie

Ukiyoto Publishing

All global publishing rights are held by

Ukiyoto Publishing

Published in 2022

Content Copyright © Mimie

ISBN 9789362690128

All rights reserved.
No part of this publication may be reproduced, transmitted, or stored in a retrieval system, in any form by any means, electronic, mechanical, photocopying, recording or otherwise, without the prior permission of the publisher.

The moral rights of the author have been asserted.

This is a work of fiction. Names, characters, businesses, places, events, locales, and incidents are either the products of the author's imagination or used in a fictitious manner. Any resemblance to actual persons, living or dead, or actual events is purely coincidental.

This book is sold subject to the condition that it shall not by way of trade or otherwise, be lent, resold, hired out or otherwise circulated, without the publisher's prior consent, in any form of binding or cover other than that in which it is published.

www.ukiyoto.com

To all my writer friends who never encouraged me because they never really knew I write.

Mimie

Princess remembered a lot of things from her past, and she smiled as she walked through her memory. Her brown locks ruffled in the air as she looked toward Manila Bay's horizon. Two empty paper cups, still wet with condensation left two circular marks on the cement ledge she sat on, as she took the trash to the bins across the bike lane. Iced coffee was the best thing there is on a sunny afternoon. But she needs to get home early, or she'll be late for work tomorrow. She wanted another cup though.

~~~

"Princess, what do you want daddy to read to you next?" She was six at the time, and story time continued until before she went into high school. "Cinderella now! We read Snow White last night, so let's do Cinderella!" She heard these fairytales every night, and had memorized their stories, yet she never grew tired of them. It fascinated her, how the princes managed to arrive at just the right time, how they saved the princesses from evil, and everything vile. Someday, she thought then, she was going to find her "knight in shining armor." Someday, someone is going to save her.

Save her from what? She had a great family who supported her throughout her school life, she had really great friends who helped her through thick or thin, her new job as an HR executive was quite enjoyable and paid fairly well, there's not much that she could really ask for! If she needed saving, it was from a currently non-existent love life. She thought that maybe at 14 or 16, she'd have had experience like Juliet with Romeo or Ariel with Prince Eric, but nothing really happened in an exclusive school if you weren't a lesbian. She waited patiently, even through college, but nobody made a move.

"Ces, let's go out together after work!" Her friend Marie invited. "I want to tell you about my latest fling before we meet up with the others. You know Jemma and Tommy, they're all about themselves."

"It's not like I have a date right?" Princess mused.

"Oh I'm sorry, if you do then by all means-"

"Shut up!"

"Oh yeah, Price will be there!" Marie grinned slyly.

Price was a year younger than Ces. Marie caught him offering a seat to no one but Ces, and she took it as a "move" toward her, and never really stopped pairing them together. "So?" Ces answered, but she couldn't help smiling as well.

Ces separated the résumés handed to her in two piles; the ones with the stamps that read "pass" and the others with the red pen marks. Occasionally, she'd find a file or two with a cute guy, and stared at their distinct jawlines and their manly brows, but she had this melody going on inside her head when she catches herself daydreaming, which she whispers in a soft sing-song voice, "Someday my prince will come", or sometimes just hums the tune in Snow White's song.

Their office wasn't strict about clothes, so her friend pushed the boundaries of corporate clothing to its limits, wearing plunging necklines, miniskirts and the like. Princess though, couldn't even look at Marie sometimes, especially when she's off-guard and showing more than she wants to, so she just made do with her favorite puffed sleeved blouse, and flowery, A-lined skirt that went well below her knees.

"Now, how are you going to get guys if you wear those clothes?" Marie retorted one time, "they might think you're up for being a nun or something!"

"What's wrong with it?" Ces defended, "I think my get-up is lovely, reminiscent of a proper lady!"

"Yeah, reminiscent of a proper lady... In the 1800's." Marie scowled.

Ces ignored Marie most of the time. She caught a glimpse of Marie while she was talking to another of her boys. She fiddled around with the miniature aliens she collected from fast food kid's meals. She never gets tired of collecting those, with all the embarrassment Ces felt from her friend ordering small, fancy servings just to get to the short-lived adrenaline rush of receiving and opening a tiny plastic bag with a badly painted cartoon character inside. Maria went for quantity, not quality. Ces observed her own neat desk, and she had but one item that stands out among the office supplies. It was a limited-edition, sixteen-point-articulation, double-jointed, ball-joint doll, in the likeness of Disney's Rapunzel, made by a famous doll maker out of resin. She outbid a medley of buyers in an online auction, and had to go all the way to the customs office near the airport, and pay a hefty tax, just to get this fully-poseable little princess. She took Rapunzel and posed her neatly over a box of tissues, and tipped her square pencil box over for a makeshift table. "You need a stamp." She put a small eraser on its hand, and then she continued with her work.

She didn't have such dolls back then. Her toys were mostly the cheap, plastic kind, but they were still just as treasured. Her books though, were quite a different story, as her dad would say, 'you'd never learn anything from toys as you would from books.' She'd feel the spines of the leather-bound, gold-leaf, engravings of her huge fairytale collection her father bought her when she was a little girl, as she picked the story her father would read to her for bedtime.

"Your majesty, my little princess, what tale would you like to hear next?" Her dad would ask, and she'd spout a title with a princess in the story, as being her namesake, those were her favorites.

It was lunch break soon enough and some of her office mates went out to eat. Ces on the other hand, went to the pantry to heat up her boxed lunch, and watch T.V. She flipped through the local channels as there was no one with her in the pantry, save for a janitress and a messenger on the corner, flirting with each other. She stopped on an old deodorant commercial, which featured a girl dropping her hanky, while a man stopped and picked it up with her. Ces' eyes grew large at the sudden inspiration she just had.

Later that evening, Marie yapped about her new fling from France even before arriving at their regularly scheduled get-together at the vegan burger joint with their former batch-mates from class, Jemma and Tommy. Ces' ears hurt from the non-stop babble she was hearing while she thought of some ways to make Price notice her. Price was late. Marie almost finished her life story when a voice from behind stopped her candy-apple-red lips.

"Sorry guys, the traffic was just intense!" Cess smiled at him. She took this moment to get her face towel and wipe her forehead. She kind of regretted not having a handkerchief with her at the time. Face towels absorb sweat more efficiently, but look less lady-like. She flung the orange towel by Price, hoping to have the same "axe-effect" moment as the commercial. She stood up and tried to get it back, while sneaking for a reaction from the guy. "Oops!" She nonchalantly exclaimed.

"Here, let m-" BANG. Their heads collided violently in a sudden upheaval.

Ces spent the evening in the corner of the room, buzzed and flushing red. She couldn't speak or even look at her friends as Jemma put an ice pack on Price's forehead and Marie fanned him while Tommy called for the nurse in the hospital. The impact was so intense that Price was rendered unconscious for a brief moment, and Marie panicked. Ces' nose bled from the impact, but was fine nevertheless. If only she was the one to black-out, things might've been different. She could've been like sleeping beauty, and maybe, she might've even been kissed. This was a nightmare. *I need to do something else.* She thought.

~~~

Princess reminisced about the fairytales her dad used to tell her long ago while she went out for lunch. She remembered how she asked for dance lessons just because all the princesses in her stories did at some point. There weren't any boys there either. She knew that she needed to get out of the T.V. For a while, as she might get weird ideas again. Marie was with her this time.

"I'm surprised you've not prepared your special diet thing today! What food are you allergic to anyway?" Marie asked before they got to the restaurant,

"Peanuts." she answered. "I don't know what it does to me, but the doctor said I'm allergic to peanuts when I was tested for allergens back when I was a kid, so I never ate any, and made sure to get lunch from home everyday."

"I guess you'd have to avoid Chinese then! Oh, I pity you, so pretty, yet so... "

"Boring?" Ces replied.

"I was gonna say complicated." Marie pursed her lips.

Ces was daydreaming. If only guys tended to like more lady-like women such as her, then she'd just wait for him endlessly, maybe in hibernation, if she needed to wait long.

"Snow White!" Ces exclaimed under her breath.

"What?" Marie asked with a weird, asymmetrical look on her face.
"I said Price wanted to get dinner with you SOME TIME, not Snow White. Where the hell did that come from?"

"Dinner? Are you and Jemma-Tommy coming?" They both called the couple that way, ever since they became a couple. Their names somehow evolved into one word.

"Why the hell are we going? You know what, as smart as you are, I can't believe how idiotic you can get! Just grab your sexiest clothes and meet with Price! Please!"

Marie pushed Ces inside the chicken restaurant across their building. Learning about Ces' allergies, she changed her mind about eating at the place beside it, where most of the food was cooked in peanut oil.

~~~

That night, as Ces rode a taxi home, her cell phone rang. It's a call from Price. "Hello?"

"Hi Ces, it's me, Price."

"Oh, Price! You know, I'm really sorr-"

"Wait! It's me who should apologize, that's why I called! I wasn't able to say anything that night since I passed out, and everyone was just all over me and... You know... Just... Sorry. Please have dinner with me on Friday, my treat, to make up for everything!" His tone was sheepish, but determined.

Thank God he doesn't hate me! She thought. Ces sighed. "Yes, sure. I mean, I'm pretty sure it was my fault, so I'll do anything you want!"

"Great! I'll meet you outside your building at the lobby after office hours. So, I'll see you then?"

"Okay!"

Ces felt like she could float all the way up to her apartment on the fourth floor. This was her second chance! It was just Wednesday, but she opened up her closet and rummaged through her things to find what she'd wear for Friday. She picked a white and blue frilled top with tiny lace ruffles on the collar and by the buttons, and a yellow balloon skirt with a white sash tied to the side. She covered up with a navy blue cardigan.

Before sleeping, she had a regular routine to watch what's on HBO, and that night, "Mrs. Doubtfire" was on. She didn't find most of the bits funny, even though this was supposed to be a wholesome comedy, especially the early parts where Robin Williams was failing his marriage with his antics in the film. He already had a perfectly fine woman in his life, and he just had to ruin it. When she got to the part where he performed a Heimlich manoeuvre on his wife's date when he got choked on a spicy bit of seafood though, her attention went full on to the scene. As it turns out, he was allergic to chilli, and his throat got swollen up inside.

"Where are we going?" Ces asked that night at Price's car while he drove.

"There's this great Asian Fusion restaurant at Timog that I tried that just blew my mind, and I'd like for you to try. I hope you like Asian cuisine..."

"I haven't really tried much Asian food because of my-" Ces paused. This could be her second chance. This could mean her first kiss. "My mom, she hates it. I'd like to try it though! Especially Chinese food!"

The whole time they were together in the car up until they reached the restaurant, they talked about their school days. Price was pretty laid back as he drove, and smiled as he talked about past years, while Princess fidgeted, laughed along nervously, and just sometimes revealed a bit of her when Price caught her off guard. A lady shouldn't laugh too hard, and be mindful of her actions in the presence of gentlemen. She stifled the little snorts she makes when she laughs, resulting in a sound that resembles a pent-up sneeze, that Price thought she had the sniffles.

When Ces and Price arrived at the restaurant, they got to know each other pretty well from all the traffic in Makati. They even talked a lot while looking for a parking spot, so Ces was pretty excited the whole time. "I didn't know there were perks to being a call center agent. From what I've heard you guys are just mostly stressed out!" Ces declared. She wasn't really all that interested in what people do in call centers, she just wanted to know more about him.

"It's because we're stressed out that we have a lot of perks." Price laughed. "Like a really good medical plan and HMO! It really helps, especially with having a really big family like mine. My younger sisters get into all sorts of trouble but are accounted for, so one of my older brothers got jealous and actually asked me for an extension for his kids!"

"Wait," Ces said, "Just how many are you in your family?"

"My immediate family? Counting my parents? Eight."

"Wow."

"I know. All I remember being in the middle is that I was always subject to the whims of my elder siblings, mostly to keep the little girls from getting the brunt of my brothers' and sister's uncontrolled force. It's cool though, it's just how they love me." Price joked.

"I wouldn't know," Ces revealed, "I'm an only child, so Jemma, Tommy and Marie are the only thing closest to brothers and sisters that I have."

Price ordered for them both. Breaded dory stir-fried in Tau-si sauce with black beans, Beef and broccoli crock-pot, Creamy Lo-mi noodles, and Custard Butchi for dessert. Ces didn't know any of the dishes they ordered, besides the beef and broccoli that was probably going to be in some kind of sauce. Beads of sweat started to form on her temples, and she wiped them off with her face towel abruptly. When the meal arrived, some new fragrances and colors attracted Ces, and she soon forgot about her uneasiness in the place.

"Jemma and Tommy were my batchmates so we played together since we were kids, even with Marie sometimes, being Tommy's cousin." Ces said, while she took a bite out of the fish.

"Small world, huh?" said Price in between chews. Does he even know that it's bad manners to talk while your mouth is full? Maybe she'd teach him when they officially become a couple.

"Yeah. We're all almost like relatives then, but how did you know Jemma-Tommy? It looks like you guys are close."

"I knew Jemma since fifth grade," Price reported, "We became neighbors when we left Cebu."

"So that means you've known them way back when Jemma and Tommy started dating?" Ces enthusiastically asked.

"Jemma and Tommy are an institution!" Price laughed as he told Ces how long they've been together. "I mean, they've been together since Jemma and I were in High school, so that must be like, eight years ago!"

"How did they get together?" Ces asked. It always is her curiosity to know how people meet and love, having never really experienced it herself.

"They fought over fish balls."

"What?"

"Fish balls. Both of them were buying fish balls, and both were claiming to be the first one in line to be served, and they fought over it. In the end, it was for some other dude so they both had to wait for their share!"

Ces couldn't understand it. How can people love someone by fighting with them? It was absurd. Suddenly, Prices eyes grew large, and his mouth stopped moving, revealing a mulch of half-chewed beef and broccoli.

"What?" Ces tried to say, but instead, she was surprised to hear nothing come out of her mouth but "mmm?" Slowly, her eyes felt heavy despite being ridiculously awake from the energy drinks she guzzled just before leaving the office. She loosened up her blouse for it was getting pretty hard to breathe. Price was calling someone frantically over his cell phone. *How rude,* She thought. They were on a perfectly fine dinner and he calls someone right in front of her, in a yell, asking for help. Help? Why? The waiters touched her face. She didn't feel anything. They held her hand, asking her if she felt all right. People were crowding over their table. Her hand looks really red, and huge. Did she get fat in five minutes? The crowds were stifling. There was a ringing in her ears, and all their voices were muffled. Her mouth wouldn't open. Suddenly, she heard an ambulance.

The next thing she knew, Jemma, Tommy and Marie were beside her. They were all in the hospital, except she didn't see Price anywhere with them. Jemma's face was almost teary from concern, and Tommy had a stern knot on his brows.

"How do you feel? Do you want anything? Water?" Jemma asked. Ces' throat was itchy, and she couldn't speak properly yet. Marie made a snort, and in contrast with Tom and Jemma, was trying to restrain her laughter. But like a wild, untamed horse, she broke loose with a held-up laugh, like a really loud snicker

"H-Haha- Have you seen yourself in the mirror?" she asked. "I'm sorry, I love you, but this is just priceless!" She took her smart phone out and held it up against Ces. After a soft, digital "click" sound, she turned her phone around so the screen faced Ces. She grabbed the phone, with her swollen hands and pressed "Delete". She thought that maybe that image was why Price was nowhere to be found.

It took a full week before Princess returned to work, even though her allergies were gone immediately the next afternoon. Even though she recognized the girl looking back at her in the mirror already, she felt really stupid to go about her tactic with a method that was so unreliable. She stayed in her pyjamas and her red, teary-eyed face that week at home, and read her favorite books. She felt like Rapunzel in her tower, only it was her will to stay in her tower, and no prince ever came.

When she did come to work that next Monday, she was greeted by the whole office, as they were all pretty concerned with her. Even Marie acted strangely, as if she was constipated or there was something that she wants to but can't get rid of. When she had the courage, she walked to Ces' cubicle and whispered, "I'm really sorry for making fun of you... And I'm not just saying this because the boss is currently giving me the evil eye everyday or anything, I just really am!"

Her face contorted in various ways as she spoke, which made Ces uncomfortably aware that she was hiding something. "Hey, Dinner's on me, let's have some fun with everyone! What do you say?"

"On a Monday?" Ces asked. This was unusual, even for Marie. "C'mon girl, I promise to be good this time!" *This time... Hmm...*

The day went smoothly, even though she noticed that some of her office mates acted a bit strange, including Marie. Some were hanging about her cubicle all the time, asking if she needed anything, one was avoiding her like she was dangerous, a few spouted into a fit of giggles as soon as they passed her cubicle, and Marie was acting paranoid, fidgeting, looking at her and avoiding her gaze, attempting to chat, then suddenly shrinking back to her own space... The flamboyant, confident Marie, shrinking? Ces knotted her brows. She felt a dark void in her heart. She couldn't make sense of it yet, but the scent of infidelity in Marie's corner was much more intensified that day.

Jemma, Tommy and Price were already there when they arrived at the vegan burger joint they frequented. Price waved with a shaky "Hey." To Ces, and she tried to smile, but couldn't look at his face.

"You're really fine now right?" Jemma affirmed.

"We were really worried about you. We didn't know what to tell the doctors until Price talked to them. Marie was the only other person who knew about it, and she was late." Tommy explained.

So that was probably why Price wasn't there in the ward! Her cheeks flushed as she sheepishly answered, "I'm fine."

"I wish you could've told me about it though, I wouldn't have insisted on the restaurant if you did," Price interjected. He looked as if he felt stupid. He must have.

"I'm sorry, I know I said I'd do anything, and I insisted, but I just didn't want to say 'no' and be a priss about it..." Ces claimed, as she looked at her weird-colored burger. It was made from banana blossoms and mushrooms, and she couldn't decide if she liked the idea or not.

"We know how you feel, and it's not entirely your fault!" Jemma tried to comfort Ces. She had the habit of saying "we" all the time, as if Tommy shared her feelings by default.

"Yeah, it's Marie's fault for sharing the pic-" Tommy started. Marie stood up so suddenly with a face akin to constipation. Tommy's eyes widened, and he bit his lip.

"You mean you haven't even TOLD her?!" Jemma loudly asked, as she slapped her forehead.

"I apologised!" Marie said in a high-pitched voice.

"She doesn't even know what for!" Jemma yelled in an even higher pitch.

"WHAT'S GOING ON?" Princess yelled. Nobody from their group has heard her yell, so everyone looked at her, astounded. Marie was even more scared now.

"W-well, I just emailed the pic, you know, the one with your face-, anyway, I sent it to the boss so he'd know about your condition, and well, I kinda sent it wrongly..."

"What? I thought I deleted that?" Ces asked, annoyed that she was being unclear.

"There were two pics, and I sent it to our team email blast, okay? I'm REALLY sorry! I swear I'm not making fun of you this time!" Marie blurted in speed.

Ces' face became redder than the tomatoes in her burger. Her officemates' actions made sense now! She ran off and went to the cafe across the street. Nothing will make her feel better than some iced coffee. She ordered, sat quietly in the corner, and sipped her chilly cup. She suddenly heard the seat across her graze the tiled floor.

She looked up, and saw Price with an uncomfortable face. "For all it's worth, I'm betting that she means it Ces. I think she's sincerely feeling sorry."

"I know, I'm just really mad, and embarrassed right now, and I just can't talk to her yet." She said.

Ces stirred her coffee and avoided Price's gaze. She's alone again with him, and she felt awkward, but determination was once again filling her heart as she sipped more of her drink.

"Marie is like my evil stepsister," she continued, "and being sisters, no matter how vile she can be, I can't help but love her."

Price chuckled at her idea. "And being Cinderella, you can't help but get into trouble, huh?" He continued.

Ces' eyes sparkled. Not only did she get inspired with another idea, she also thought Price was actually thinking of her as a real fairytale princess.

"You know what, maybe I'm being too mean to Marie. I should just go and apologize." Ces was almost done with her coffee, and got up.

"Good girl." Said Price.

Ces went straight to the counter to pay for her coffee, took all the money from her pocket save for a twenty, and left her pink, flowery wallet on the counter. This would give Price an excuse to come and find her again when he discovers it, and who knows, maybe they'd get to go on a date where nothing would go wrong! Besides, the thing is unique enough to top Cinderella's shoe, plus her ID was inside, so it's all safe! They were the only ones in the cafe too. She went back out, but didn't go to the burger joint. She just took the bus home and watched her movie. All she needs to do now is to wait for Price.

The next day, Ces got into her usual routine of getting up early to fix her outfit, taking a cold shower, dressing up, cooking her meal and grabbing her bag to go to work. She moved like a haggard old hag while she did all these, since she doesn't feel awake until she actually ate breakfast at the office pantry. She rode a bus to Makati which took approximately an hour with all the traffic during rush hour, and took the elevator to the 30th floor of the newly-renovated building her office was in. At the doorway was a sensor and a keypad for all the employees to swipe their ID and passkey to time-in and enter the facility. Ces became awake now. She couldn't get in and started to bang on the nearly sound proof office to see if anyone was there to let her in.

She called Price. Surely he'd found her wallet. It was right at the counter! She swiped through her phone until she found his number, and waited for him to answer. Why wouldn't he answer? She started to get worried. Suddenly, she heard loud, clacky footsteps coming toward her. It was Marie.

"Ces? Why are you outside?" She asked.

Ces didn't want to talk to her yet, but she needed to go in or she'd be late. "I left my wallet at the cafe yesterday, and Price might've found it." She answered, still holding the phone against her cheek.

"It's Price's day off today! He might still be sleeping. Come, I'll just write a note on the reception desk about your time-in. It's hot out here!" Marie invited.

Ces had no choice but to agree with Marie this time. She went into the office and did what she could without going out. If she went out, she was sure that she wouldn't be able to come back in. Maybe Price has her wallet, but was just waiting for the right time to come to the rescue.

Price never did come though, and it was 30 minutes past 6pm already, and it started to rain. Ces tried to call Price again. Maybe he just forgot about it. Finally, there was an answer. "Hello?" came the raspy sounding voice.

"Price? Are you okay?" asked Ces. He didn't sound too good.

"Princess? Was that you who was calling the whole time? Sorry, I was sleeping. It's my day off today, and I just ran a double shift after our get-together yesterday so I was trying to catch on some z's. What's up?"

"Oh, sorry, it's just that, um, have you seen my wallet? I think I left it at the cafe when we ate out yesterday, and I thought that being the last person there, maybe you've seen it on the table or the counter?" Ces couldn't sort out what she was trying to say much. She tried calling Price a number of times throughout the day since she was unsure of when he'd wake up. She didn't know he'd be so tired today.

"Nope, sorry. I didn't really order anything, so I just got up and left. Maybe it's with the manager or something. I can go and check if you want, it's kind of nearby." Price offered.

"Could you? Oh, that's so kind of you!" Ces exclaimed. She was glad Price was such a gentleman. She got excited that she'd get to see him again later too.

"I'll bring it to your office if I find it. You are still in the office, right? I'll call you if I do." Price sounded genuinely concerned, but still kind of sleepy.

"Yes, thank you! You are a life saver!" Ces thought it was so convenient for the cafe to be near Price's apartment. She hadn't even thought of that little detail. It was pretty easy enough for him that he had a car.

Ces waited at the lobby for Price's call. Meanwhile, the rain was still pouring. Marie just got out of the office for overtime, and saw Ces flipping through a magazine and checking her cell phone. "Ces? What are you still doing here?" she asked.

"I'm waiting for Price. He found my wallet." Ces said coldly.

"That's nice. Listen Ces, I hope you're not still mad at me or anything, I really didn't mean to be so... mean!" Marie apologized.

"Thanks, and I'm sorry too, for being really stubborn about the whole thing." Ces finally gave in. She was too excited about meeting Price tonight that she couldn't really hold a grudge against Marie anymore.

"Well, I'll leave the two of you to your own thing now!" Marie winked, as she eyed a silhouette coming in from the doorway. She walked out with her clacketty heels at the opposite exit.

Princess stood up at the sight of Price at the doorway. He was soaking wet and shivering when he went into the lobby. She ran toward him with her face towel and attempted to dry his hair and face with it without thinking. "Oh my god, why are you so wet?" she asked.

"As you can see, it started pouring." Price sarcastically said, with his hand showing the view from the large glass windows.

"Yeah, but you have a car, don't you?" Ces said worriedly. Her face towel was soaking, and she couldn't think of where she could wring the thing, so she just did it on the artificial plant's pot beside the sofa. Both of them sat down while Ces now tried to wipe his shoulders.

Price grabbed her frantic hand and took the small towel to dry himself up. "Coding." He plainly stated. He took the pink, flowery wallet out of his pocket and handed it over quickly to Ces. It looked awkward in his huge, bony hands, and he knew it.

"I'm so sorry, if I knew, I'd have just gone there myself!" Ces cried. Price's head rested on her shoulder. Her heart beat faster that moment, and she savored his warm cheek against her skin. She thought about how they even got to that romantic moment at all. Did he feel good that he's saved the day for her, or did he just pity Ces for her helplessness? That lasted about five seconds, until her shoulders started to burn. She spied on his flushed face and saw that his chest was heaving. Her heart beat even faster from the frantic realization she had that Price had fainted from having an extremely high fever.

~~~

Princess held his hand inside the ward. He was still hot, although the IV made sure he maintained a decent enough temperature. She didn't know who to call in such situations, and couldn't, for the life of her, reach into his pocket to get his wallet and view his emergency contact in his ID. It was her fault that everything happened anyway, so she stayed. After a few hours, Price turned his head and saw her clasped onto his hand. Her head was down, so she couldn't see his face smile, then ever so slowly, evolve into a melancholic expression.

"Ces," he called. Ces looked up. Her eyes were wide, surprised that he was awake that time of night. "I like you Ces." He said. But before Princess could even answer, he added, "You're like my little sister, always getting me into trouble. When you get a boyfriend, make sure you introduce him to me, okay?" he smiled. "Sure," Ces managed to smile as tears ran down her face. She was so relieved to find Price recovering, and she felt a burning spell cast on her chest. "But don't go scaring him away okay?"

Price already called one of his brothers to come and stay with him in the hospital that night, so Ces left when he came. She walked the lonely streets of Makati, eventually finding an ordinary bus whizzing by, and got on. She didn't feel scared even if the bus lurched from side to side with every turn, or when she went forward and knocked her head on the seat in front of her when it hit the brakes. She could die that evening, but it didn't feel like it mattered.

She skipped her routine movie that night, and called up Marie. Marie could hear her sobbing at the end of the line, and waited for her to speak up.

"Am I ugly Marie? Am I that ugly that no guy wants to date me?" She was crying so hard that she didn't hear Marie say "Hold on, I'm coming to your place" at the end of the line. She just hung up the phone and went to her room. She went under her thick comforter and hugged one of her dolls, half expecting to die in there from suffocation. It wasn't even 30 minutes before she heard a loud screech of the brakes on Marie's compact car. She rushed over to Ces' room and flipped over her comforter. Marie hugged her friend tightly and whispered "You're not ugly, you're beautiful!" over and over, until Princess calmed down.

"It isn't hard to attract men you know," Marie said when Ces asked how she does it. "It's the keeping him part that's tough." She sighed.

Ces didn't think Marie wanted to actually keep any of the guys she's dated, but apparently that was the case. She thought Marie was a guy expert, being with so many of them already. Now she was beginning to doubt her initial idea. "Anyway, the key is knowing how and when to flirt." Marie taught.

"Flirt?" Ces winced at the idea.

"Of course!" Marie exclaimed, annoyed that Ces would even question her foolproof techniques. "A subtle swish of the hips as you walk, a certain glance in his direction, a bat of an eyelash every now and then in the middle of a conversation..." she enumerated as she demonstrated her usual routines for hooking up.

"And if I do those things, guys will like me?" Ces couldn't believe her ears.

Her monotonous tone rubbed Marie the wrong way. "Hey, don't believe me if you don't want to, you're the one-"

Ces grabbed Marie's arm and gave in, "All right, all right, fine, just-teach me. But I'm not going so far as to show cleavage or anything like you do, okay?"

"Of course, that's MY style." Claimed Marie.

~~~

Both of them spent the whole night like high-school kids in a sleepover, with Marie teaching her wiles to her protégé. When the sun came up, they remembered that they still had work that next morning, but decided to skip and call in sick.

Marie opened up Princess' wardrobe flamboyantly, as if she was opening some grand window curtains. "Umm... This might take a while."

"What will?" Ces asked, still wearing the comforter over her head like a matryoshka doll. Her eyes were bleary and swelling red from all the drama of the previous night. They barely even slept, but Marie was awake as ever.

"CLOTHES." Mouthed Marie. "I mean, there's nothing remotely sexy here that'd fit the classiest bar I know! Well let me see..." Marie rummaged through the whole closet, picking out the stuff that hung at the far sides, the ones that were barely or practically never worn. One of them was a dance dress, made way back when Princess was still in the Dance organization at their college. She only kept it as a souvenir.

"That will not even fit me anymore," she interrupted Marie's rummaging, "I did grow some boobs, just not as humongous as yours!" Ces laughed. It felt refreshing, after a whole night of sobbing relentlessly.

"I'm just picking out some options!" Marie pointed out. "How about this one?" she asked. She held up a purple shirt-dress with cropped sleeves, which had two, black, 'S'-shaped lines on each side that accentuated the body's curves.

"That one's nice, I could pair it with a nice set of leggi-"

"I thought you should wear it bare-legged, with a nice pair of boots!" Marie quipped.

Eventually, after a bit of childish squabbling, Ces agreed to wear the shirt-dress, with the condition that she could wear a pair of shorts underneath. After freshening up, Marie got a pair of black, heeled booties from the bottom of the closet, which were good as new, and never been worn. She helped Ces wear the dress, and then she let her borrow a knitted, drape bolero she had in her huge, overnight bag and styled Princess' hair up. "Oh-em-gee, you look like a character from a Korean novella!" she cried and clapped in accomplishment.

"I feel weird with my thighs showing..." complained Ces.

"Eh, you'll get used to it! C'mon! We just HAVE to go out with you in this! Let me just fix myself for a while."

~~~

Marie continued to fix herself up inside the taxi they were in. Ces kept shifting her skirt down and shimmying this way and that. The huge drop-earrings hung heavily on her earlobes and started to hurt. She gazed at Marie as she applied some eyeliner while the taxi was moving. It was a miracle how she managed not to poke her eye out.

"Just take a left here and we'll get down at Empire." She directed the driver in-between swipes of her 'candy-apple-red' lipstick. Marie finished painting her face just in time. "We're here!" she turned to Ces and smiled with an eyebrow up.

They pull over at a place with high, tan-washed walls, and Ces could barely see anything except from the numerous lights above. It started raining slightly, and they both ran toward the shade having forgotten to bring umbrellas. The entrance sat beneath an awkward corner, where a bored bouncer checked people out and took tickets. Marie had all kinds of tickets in her bag, and rummaged through its pockets until she found the right one. Ces' brows met nervously. "Don't worry," whispered Marie, "and follow my lead!"

"Hi Dong!" Marie flounced over the bouncer with a sing-song voice. Badong smiled.

"Rie, hey girl!" he responded, gently reaching for her hand. Marie handed her hand over and let the huge man caress it with his fingers.

"Hey listen, I got a ticket now, but my friend over there, the one in purple, it's her first time here and she wants to try first, so is it okay if I just sneak her in for just a bit?"

Marie leaned over to let him have a full view of her cleavage, and bent her head to the side, biting her lip. "I promise it'll be just this once, and we won't make trouble!"

Badong took a glimpse of her chest with a gaping mouth, but caught himself and tried to look elsewhere. He scratched his head as he tried to comprehend what this pretty girl was trying to say.

"Uhh, you'll get me in big trouble again!" he kindly exclaimed.

"C'mon Dongski..." Marie pleaded in a cutesy voice.

"O-okay, just-just don't get me in trouble okay! Quickly now!" Badong was clearly stricken with Marie's charms. Princess' eyes were wide with amazement and fear. How could she ever accomplish something like that?

As they entered the gate, they walked amidst tables and people that smelled of cigarettes and Chico fruit. Christmas lights hung around the trees and shrubs in the middle of June, and waiters all paced quickly holding trays with bucketfuls of beer and fancy cocktail glasses.

"And that's how you do it!" Marie exclaimed when they were far enough from Badong as they were.

"This time," she said, "It's your turn to hook someone up! Remember what I taught you!" she nudged Ces as they entered the indoor space.

Ces found herself being pushed into a dark room. When her eyes adjusted, she saw a flood of people chattering all over the sides, holding a few drinks. Strobe lights flickered from the corners of the room, and multi-colored beams flashed from above. Mist from the smoke machines hissed and lingered on the bottom-lit stage in the center of the area.

"Why don't we order a drink first?" Ces smiled hesitantly. Marie shook her head in disapproval.

"U-uh, you have to get a drink the OTHER way!" she emphasized.

Ces sighed. As soon as Marie found a spot for them to hang out, loud music started to blare from the overhead speakers. People started dancing everywhere, and Ces couldn't find Marie as she was pushed toward the fluorescent stage. It was better when she was up there, as she had leverage, and a lot of the other people didn't seem to want to go on it. She leaned on a pole and tip-toed to find her friend, when suddenly, she heard a burble and felt vibrations stemming from the pole she was leaning on.

A loud *FSHHH!* Sound came as a huge foam of bubbles came spraying out from all the poles surrounding the stage. Ces was instantly covered with the wet, soapy fluff.

She started to wipe her shoulders and her front, and a waiter came out of nowhere handing her a drink. He mouthed off the direction where it came from, but Ces, being less than average in height, couldn't distinguish where it was from.

Apparently, there was a certain grace to her movements that an observant guy somewhere thought she was actually dancing. She decided to just raise her glass, drink the whole thing and wipe off more of the soap that was clinging to her body, not even thinking about how she got the drink in the first place. Suddenly, another girl started to imitate her movements as if to mock her, although she did this in tune to the distinct beats coming from the speakers. Ces took this as an offense. How dare this slut make fun of her in front of all these people!

Ces was furious, and her warm body felt so light and floaty that she could almost do anything. She felt angry and brave after that drink, and she wanted more of it. She tried one of Marie's tricks this time, slowly caressing off a bit of foam on her waist while gracefully moving forward and up. Those moves in dance class were clearly showing their worth. Two more different shots came from nowhere. She raised both glasses and drank one after the other.

This time, the other girl, the curly haired bitch teasing her, started to shake her soaked breasts wildly, spattering some foam all over the place. Wild cheers went out as men ogled at her movements. This was the last straw. Princess let her hair loose and flipped it around to the foam, and flung it toward the girl. The crowd grew wild, as four more drinks came one after the other, while Ces drank each one without reserve. A few moments later, Ces started to feel sick. She headed toward the door as she tried one last attempt to find Marie. Finally she saw her! There she was in a dark corner, kissing a guy.

As the contempt and acid tried to force its way up her throat, she managed to run out and reach the outside corner where she couldn't help herself any longer and released all the bile and alcohol she clearly couldn't manage.

As she swept her hair up, she noticed that she was looking at a leather shoe, covered with her stomach fluid. She suddenly propped up and her head almost hit a man's face. "Whoa!" he said. His face was covered in stubble, and he had thick eyebrows.

"Oh my god! I'm so sorry for your shoe! Here, let me-" she managed to say. Her speech was slurred, and she knew she was drunk. She was never really used to having so much alcohol in one night. She reached for the face towel in her bag and reached down to wipe the man's shoe.

The guy was really surprised. "It's fine! I'll do it! I have tiss-" and BAM. Both of them fell down on their bottoms holding their heads. It was extremely lucky none of them hit the fresh spew on the floor.

Ces got up first. She clearly dealt the harder blow. She reached out her hand and asked him, "Are you okay?" while holding her own forehead, while still having a little yellowish-greenish droplet of vileness just right by her cherry-scented lip-gloss. She finally noticed the smell and wiped it off.

Sam, as she was told his name later on, looked up and saw a girl, slightly silhouetted by the bright glare of the streetlamp that formed a halo directly above her. She helped him get up, and he wiped his shoes with some pocket tissues he had in his pocket, and threw them out at the bin just by the lamp. He noticed Ces leaning on the wall on the corner, and helped her sit down by the gutter while he sat beside her. "Are you okay?" he asked.

"I didn't see you, sorry..." Ces sheepishly slurred.

"It's okay, these aren't mine." Sam quipped, looking at his slightly wet shoes. Ces cackled at his joke. Sam looked at Ces puzzled for a bit, and realized that he made a joke unknowingly and laughed with her awkwardly. "I'm Sam by the way, what's yours?" he asked.

Before he could even correct his mistake, Ces started to laugh even harder. Sam's face flushed redder than the drunken blush Princess had. "I'm Princess." She giggled. "No, I mean, what's your name?"

"My name IS Princess!" she emphasized.

"Oooh, I thought you said you're a-, Never mind." Sam shamefully put his hand over his face.

Ces observed this guy make blunder after blunder with his awkward demeanor, and decided that he looked adorable in it. Maybe it was just how the alcohol messed with her head, but she liked how she didn't overthink things right now. "Want to date a princess?"

~~~

Marie looked for Ces inside the club, but she couldn't find her anywhere. She was worried that some lecher might've scooped her off and took advantage of her, and was starting to feel really guilty for not looking after her friend as soon as a cute guy was all over her. She thought Ces was enjoying herself much already by the bubble stage, and was clearly getting the hang of things, when she suddenly just disappeared! She looked in the restrooms, and out in the smoking area, where she never thought Ces would hang out since she hated the smell of tobacco.

She slipped outside the gate to look, and almost stepped on some strong, pungent gunk by the corner when she found Ces sitting on the gutter, with her arm huddled over a guy. Marie smiled slyly as she slowly crept back toward the club. She was about to turn when she saw a truck whizz past the rain-soaked pavement, and called out "CES, WATCH OUT!"

Ces heard a whizz pass by her, and before she could even hear Marie's warning, she grabbed Sam's shoulder and pushed him back towards the wall. He landed really close to the spew on the corner, but managed to keep his hand from leaning on it. Ces on the other hand, was soaked with the murky brackish water that sprayed all over her back. After a while, she heard Sam whisper, "You saved me!"

~~~

Marie went back to the office the next morning, and gave their boss a doctor's note. It says there that Princess has suffered an allergic reaction due to ingesting food containing peanut oil. Luckily, the man couldn't read much of what it says on the note, and didn't notice the date and time on the piece of paper. Ces was out again today, and although Marie didn't know where she was, she knew who she was with.

It was sunset at Manila Bay, and Ces ran toward Sam who walked ahead toward the cafe. "Wait up!" she called, right after throwing the two previous paper cups of iced coffee away. Sam stopped and looked back at the better dressed girl she was with than from the previous night. His hair swept from the back as the wind blew, and the sun shone on his face revealing a nice big smile. A halo formed from the light that glared behind his Princess.

About the Author

Mimie

Mimie has been working as an artist professionally for 11 years and only wrote as a hobby since she was 8. If this book sells then she might have more confidence in herself.

www.ingramcontent.com/pod-product-compliance
Lightning Source LLC
LaVergne TN
LVHW041601070526
838199LV00046B/2079